This book belongs to

....

CONTENTS

Rupert and the Bosun's Chair: Story originated and illustrated by Stuart Trotter
Text and couplets written by Beth Harwood. Designed by Martin Aggett

Endpapers adapted from the *Rupert Annual,* 1966, illustrated by ALFRED BESTALL

THE
RUPERT
ANNUAL

EXPRESS NEWSPAPERS

EGMONT
We bring stories to life

Published in Great Britain 2012 by Egmont UK Limited
239 Kensington High Street, London W8 6SA
Rupert Bear™ & © 2012 Classic Media Distribution Limited/Express Newspapers.
All Rights Reserved.

ISBN 978 1 4052 6341 2
51510/1
Printed in Italy

No. 77

RUPERT'S LUNAR CALENDAR 2013

A lunar calendar is special, as it will tell you when to expect the different phases of the moon.

January

Mo	Tu	We	Th	Fr	Sa	Su
	1	2	3	4	5	6
7	8	9	10	11	12	13
14	15	16	17	18	19	20
21	22	23	24	25	26	27
28	29	30	31			

February

Mo	Tu	We	Th	Fr	Sa	Su
				1	2	3
4	5	6	7	8	9	10
11	12	13	14	15	16	17
18	19	20	21	22	23	24
25	26	27	28			

March

Mo	Tu	We	Th	Fr	Sa	Su
				1	2	3
4	5	6	7	8	9	10
11	12	13	14	15	16	17
18	19	20	21	22	23	24
25	26	27	28	29	30	31

April

Mo	Tu	We	Th	Fr	Sa	Su
1	2	3	4	5	6	7
8	9	10	11	12	13	14
15	16	17	18	19	20	21
22	23	24	25	26	27	28
29	30					

May

Mo	Tu	We	Th	Fr	Sa	Su
		1	2	3	4	5
6	7	8	9	10	11	12
13	14	15	16	17	18	19
20	21	22	23	24	25	26
27	28	29	30	31		

June

Mo	Tu	We	Th	Fr	Sa	Su
					1	2
3	4	5	6	7	8	9
10	11	12	13	14	15	16
17	18	19	20	21	22	23
24	25	26	27	28	29	30

July

Mo	Tu	We	Th	Fr	Sa	Su
1	2	3	4	5	6	7
8	9	10	11	12	13	14
15	16	17	18	19	20	21
22	23	24	25	26	27	28
29	30	31				

August

Mo	Tu	We	Th	Fr	Sa	Su
			1	2	3	4
5	6	7	8	9	10	11
12	13	14	15	16	17	18
19	20	21	22	23	24	25
26	27	28	29	30	31	

September

Mo	Tu	We	Th	Fr	Sa	Su
						1
2	3	4	5	6	7	8
9	10	11	12	13	14	15
16	17	18	19	20	21	22
23	24	25	26	27	28	29
30						

October

Mo	Tu	We	Th	Fr	Sa	Su
	1	2	3	4	5	6
7	8	9	10	11	12	13
14	15	16	17	18	19	20
21	22	23	24	25	26	27
28	29	30	31			

November

Mo	Tu	We	Th	Fr	Sa	Su
				1	2	3
4	5	6	7	8	9	10
11	12	13	14	15	16	17
18	19	20	21	22	23	24
25	26	27	28	29	30	

December

Mo	Tu	We	Th	Fr	Sa	Su
						1
2	3	4	5	6	7	8
9	10	11	12	13	14	15
16	17	18	19	20	21	22
23	24	25	26	27	28	29
30	31					

Key:

New Moon: . . . .

First quarter moon: . . .

Full Moon: . . . .

Last quarter moon: . . .

Unfortunately, a lunar calendar won't tell you when a blue moon might appear! Learn more about the mysterious blue moon in the first story.

RUPERT

and the
BLUE MOON

IN THIS STORY
YOU CAN READ ABOUT —

 The old man who lives at Witch End Green

Mrs Bear who needs a Christmas-tree fairy

A surprise visitor who calls at night-time

And two children everyone would like to meet!

From The Rupert Book, *1956. Illustrated by* Alfred Bestall.

RUPERT WANTS A SPILL-HOLDER

"I haven't bought the presents yet,"
Sighs Rupert. "Now, what shall I get?"

"I need some spills," says Mr Bear, ★
For he can find no matches there.

The question Rupert wants to ask
Must wait till Mummy's done her task.

"Perhaps the villagers nearby
Can help me," Rupert thinks. "I'll try!"

It is Christmas Eve and Rupert still can't decide what presents to give his mummy and daddy. "I wish I knew how to find out what people want without asking them," he thinks. Strolling into the next room he finds his daddy standing by the fire and looking rather glum. "There are no matches," says Mr Bear. "I can't light my pipe. If only we had some spills and something to keep them in, matches wouldn't be needed." Rupert keeps silent.

"Surely that's one idea for me!" he thinks as he wanders away. "I wonder what sort of a thing is best to keep spills in," he ponders. "Maybe I'll go and find Mummy and talk to her. Perhaps she will drop a hint without knowing it, just as Daddy did. Hello, she's just going shopping. I shall have to wait until she gets back. I know what I'll do! I'll see if anybody in the next village can tell me what a spill-holder is." And off he trots towards Witch End Green.

A spill is a thin piece of wood or paper used to light a log fire.

So first of all he makes a stop
To see what's in the old man's shop.

"This money's all that I have got,
I can't afford to pay a lot."

The shopman smiles, and with a nod,
Agrees the vase is very odd.

"That's one thing settled, very soon!
But please, where is this strange blue moon?"

On reaching the village Rupert makes a bee-line for his favourite shop, the one that is always so full of treasures and queer old things. So many interesting objects are in the window that he almost forgets what he is looking for, but at length he goes inside. "Please, this is all the money I've got, and I want something to hold spills for my daddy," he says. The old shopman smiles gently. "All sorts of things will hold spills. Let's both look!" he suggests. Gazing round the crowded shelves Rupert spies a strangely shaped pot. "What a nice vase! Could I have that?" he asks. "Aye, 'tis odd indeed," chuckles the old man. "You'd only find this sort of thing once in a blue moon. In fact, I've never seen another like it. However, none of my other customers seems to have wanted it, so you shall have it." "Oh, thank you," says Rupert. "Does that mean it's very rare? And, please, where is the blue moon? Is it very far away?"

RUPERT TAKES HIS GIFT HOME

"I'll hold it with the greatest care,
And go straight home," says Rupert Bear.

"If someone's here, I'll have to wait,"
Breathes Rupert, creeping through the gate.

"I must see what it looks like here,
For in the shop it looked so queer."

He hears a hiss, and gasps, "What's that?"
Then turns and gazes at the cat.

At Rupert's question the old man laughs aloud and pats him on the head. Then, still chuckling quietly, he packs up the parcel but doesn't give him an answer. So Rupert thanks him, and, clutching his purchase tightly, he runs back to Nutwood. "I don't want anyone to see me taking it in," he thinks. "If they do, it won't be a surprise!" He creeps in cautiously and doesn't notice that Dinkie, the black cat, is standing behind him and wondering why he is behaving so strangely. Going in softly, Rupert listens. "Good!" he whispers. "There's no one else at home. I must have a peep at this thing and see if it's as nice now as it was in the shop. My, it looks quainter here than it did there!" As he gets up to take off his scarf a hissing noise makes him turn. "Goodness, where did *you* come from?" he cries. For Dinkie has silently followed him into the room and now stands with arched back, staring at the piece of pottery as if afraid of it.

RUPERT BREAKS THE ORNAMENT

At once the sparks begin to fly,
As Dinkie gives a startled cry.

The tingles shoot up Rupert's arm,
But do not cause him any harm.

"Oh dear!" he cries. "My vase has crashed,
And every bit of it is smashed!

My present's gone. What can I do?
For I've spent all my money, too!"

Rupert gazes at the cat and the oddest things start to happen. As Dinkie gives a little growl sparks begin to fly between his fur and the spill-holder on the ground. Immediately the black cat leaps in the air and then onto a box near the window, and to Rupert's astonishment the ornament rises in the air after him. Pulling himself together, Rupert dashes across to grab it. "Oo, ow! This thing is sending tingles up my arm!" he gasps. "It must be magic!" Tingling shocks start shooting from the strange objecet right up to Rupert's shoulder. "What *has* happened?" he whispers. "Has the black cat put electricity into it?" At that the thing jerks out of his hand and next instant it is lying shattered to pieces on the floor. "Oh, Daddy's present!" he moans. "What *can* I do? I could never get another one like it. And I've no money left anyway." Trying hard to keep back his tears, he fetches a brush and dustpan and sweeps up the bits.

RUPERT WONDERS ABOUT DINKIE

"The vase itself was strange enough,
But what on earth's this powdery stuff?"

He thinks, "I may find out one day,
So I won't throw the bits away."

"I'll hide the pieces just in case,
A drawer will be the very place."

But Rupert gazes at the floor,
As Dinkie rushes through the door.

Rupert looks carefully at the broken china. "There's some powdery stuff among these bits," he murmurs. Going out, he sees that Dinkie is still excited and is dancing around a patch on the carpet. "There's something extraordinary going on!" he mutters. "I won't throw these pieces away yet. I don't believe that ornament was made of ordinary china at all." He fetches a paper bag and, tipping all the bits out of the dustpan into it, he takes them to his own room. The little bear hides the paper bag at the back of the drawer among his clothes, and listens in case his parents come back. Then he returns to the other room. "I can't think what is wrong with that cat," he cries. For Dinkie is still frisking and spitting around something on the ground. "Don't be silly. It's only a little powder from that broken ornament," says Rupert. "I must have spilled it out of the dustpan!" As he bends down to scoop it up, Dinkie bolts out of the door.

RUPERT HAS A SUDDEN FRIGHT

"There must be something Dinkie feared,
Or he would not have disappeared.

What can have made this brilliant light?"
Cries Rupert, jumping back in fright.

"Whew! This has given me a scare,"
Exclaims the startled little bear.

"I've got the things for Christmas here,
So help me to unpack them, dear!"

Rupert looks for Dinkie but the black cat has disappeared. Then he looks at the powder in his hand. "There's no need to keep this," he thinks. And he tosses it into the fire. The next moment he starts back in fright, for at once a brilliant light glows from the fireplace – pink, orange and yellow, and coloured stars and sparks come fizzing out, and go crackling and swirling around the room. He topples over and covers his face, expecting every minute to be hit by something.

When Rupert opens his eyes the coloured lights and sparks and stars have swirled away out of the window. "Whew! What *was* that thing I bought?" he breathes. Just then he hears his mummy's step outside and he runs to look out, expecting that she, too, has seen the sparks. However, she seems to have noticed nothing and marches along briskly. "Hello, Rupert!" she calls. "I've had such a successful shopping day – nearly everything for Christmas!"

RUPERT MEETS THE SPARK-MAN

"There was one thing I couldn't see,
A fairy for our Christmas tree!"

Says Rupert as the curtain flaps,
"Oh, what was that? – the wind, perhaps."

A glowing shape lights up the dark.
It looks exactly like a spark!

The stranger says, "Now tell me why
You set us free, and made us fly!"

Rupert waits for an opportunity to tell his mummy of the weird things that have been happening to him, but she is in a very cheerful mood, bustling about and chattering happily while she works. "There's only one thing that I've failed to get," she says, "and that's a fairy for the top of the Christmas tree. Otherwise everything will be lovely." So Rupert hangs up his stocking and goes to bed with his story still untold. All at once his bedroom seems to quiver and his curtain flaps. Rupert doesn't know whether he is really asleep or not. A new, cold light is shining and suddenly a slender figure appears on his bedrail. For a moment, the pair stare at each other in silence. Then Rupert finds his voice. "Surely you're a ... aren't you one of those wonderful sparks?" he quavers. "Quite right," squeaks the other. "Didn't you notice that I stayed while the others swirled away? And I'm here to ask what you've been playing at!"

RUPERT IS TOLD TO MAKE HASTE

So Rupert tries to tell his friend
About the vase he cannot mend.

"Bad luck," the spark-man squeaks, "indeed!
Another vase is what you need."

He says a magic word aloud,
And soon appears a little cloud.

"Quick!" cries the spark-man. "Hurry, do!
Or I shall be no use to you."

Trying to get over his astonishment at the little stranger, Rupert scrambles out of bed, fetches the paper bag from its hiding-place, and shows him the broken pieces. "I did so want this for my daddy's present," he says, "but it broke and I can't get another. The shopman said one can find it only once in a blue moon." "Quite right again!" says the spark-man, looking amused, "or in this case twice in a blue moon. Yes, I know where that china thing came from!"

Rupert looks so mystified that the spark-man laughs again. "You didn't notice that your vase had a secret pocket, did you? In it was some Wishing Powder and it all got spilt. Look, most of it is in this bag!" He takes a pinch and tosses it up, saying a magic word, and a small cloud forms near his head. Then, all at once, he becomes very alert. "Hurry up, hurry up! Get your dressing-gown on, little bear," he orders. "I like you, and perhaps I can help you."

RUPERT FLOATS ON HIS EIDERDOWN

"You guessed it was a magic pot,
And should have wished, but you did not!"

"What's happened to my eiderdown?"
Gasps Rupert with a puzzled frown.

And then he aadds, "I wish I knew
Why I must go away with you."

The spark-man answers, "Wait and see!
You want a vase, so trust in me."

Back on the bed, the spark-man goes on explaining. "You guessed it was a magic pot," he says. "You should have handled it more respectfully. And you should always wish hard when you throw Wishing Powder on a fire. You didn't, so you got nothing, though you did release us. Because of this, I'll show you something else. Hold tight!" He sprinkles more powder, and coloured clouds suddenly appear, while the eiderdown, with Rupert on it, is lifted up and carried into them!

In a moment, Rupert's room has vanished, and he is deep in the cloud. "We must be moving fast," he says. "Why are you taking me away?" "Well, you wanted another of those ornaments for your daddy, didn't you?" the spark-man answers. "So wait and see!" Rupert looks thoughtful. "But those are only found once in a blue moon," he says. "Do you mean that ..." Suddenly they leave the cloud and float through a brilliant starlit sky.

RUPERT SEES A CASTLE AHEAD

Across the brilliant starlit sky
The eiderdown goes floating by.

And soon the two are drifting near
A fairy castle, sparkling clear.

The friends have reached their journey's end,
And to the castle floor descend.

Then Rupert sees, to his great joy,
A friendly little girl and boy.

The floating eiderdown travels on amid stars even more brilliant. "Those look like the stars that shot out of my own fire when I threw Wishing Powder into it," says Rupert. "Quite right!" says the spark-man for the third time. "They've come home, and so have I. There's my home! Doesn't it look lovely?" Ahead of them, out of the night, there rises a fairy castle with shimmering pale green turrets soaring into the sky. Steadily and more slowly, Rupert is carried on towards it. Very gently the strange craft floats straight through a doorway into the castle. "Oh, how wonderful!" whispers Rupert. "And to think that the Wishing Powder has brought us all this way!" They land on a smooth polished floor, and once more he finds the air filled with pale, swirling coloured lights. Through them, he sees a little girl and a little boy standing quietly together. But the spark-man dances away. "Stay here! I won't be long!" he calls.

RUPERT UNDERSTANDS AT LAST

Here Rupert's greeted with a smile,
The girl hopes he will stay awhile.

At first it all seems strange, and so
He's shown the place where flowers grow.

"Blue Moonshine Land, we call this place,
We cannot see the Blue Moon's face."

Says Rupert, "Yes, I understand
Now I have seen your strange new land."

The little girl then steps forward. "We're *so* glad you've come to see us," she says politely. "Can we do anything for you? Would you like to see our conservatory? Look, aren't these perfect flowers! There are none like them anywhere. You only find them once in a blue moon!" "B-but why are they all here?" says Rupert, "and what is this place?" "Oh, don't you know where you are?" replies the child kindly. "This *is* the blue moon!" Seeing Rupert's astonishment, the little girl leads him out to a balcony under the stars. "We call this the land of the Blue Moon, but that's not quite right," she says. "It should really be the land of the Blue Moonshine! No one has seen the Blue Moon, only its light. It's always hiding behind another, darker moon." And peering over the rail, Rupert sees, low down in the sky, a dark object surrounded by a weird blue glow. "Now I begin to understand!" he cries as they go back.

RUPERT ENJOYS A NICE MEAL

The boy says, as he brings a tray,
"It's time you had a meal today."

They both lead Rupert to a chair,
And make him very cosy there.

The little bear feels happy now,
And asks them questions why and how.

"Come!" cries the spark-man in great haste.
"Quick, Rupert! There's no time to waste."

Rupert's excitement is growing. "That spark-man must have brought me here because there may be another spill-holder here for my daddy's Christmas present!" Before the child can reply, the little boy appears carrying a tray. "You must be hungry and thirsty," he says, "and aren't you tired? Will you let us make you comfortable?" And in a few minutes Rupert is nestling among cushions, eating a delicious meal and thinking that he has never enjoyed himself so much.

When the meal is finished, Rupert kneels up and looks at his new friends. "I think you're the nicest people I've ever met!" he smiles. "Do tell me, what are your names? And what are you doing here?" At that moment a loud noise by his ear startles him. The spark-man has returned. "Come on, come on! There's no time to waste!" he squeaks. "We must get on before it's too late!" The two children politely back away as Rupert leaves with the spark-man.

RUPERT HURRIES TO A ROOM

"Please tell me, if you do not mind,
About those two, who were so kind."

"There's no time, Rupert, to explain!
For we must hurry on again."

"Look there! The moon is sinking low,
That means Blue Moonshine Land must go."

They dash through halls, it is not far
Before they reach a door ajar.

Rupert is still inquisitive, and before going far, he turns to his companion. "Do tell me who those kind children are," he begs. "Can't you guess?" asks the spark-man. "They are a perfect little girl and a perfect little boy. They are always polite, and always clean and tidy, and never late, and never greedy and – well – they're the sort of children you only find once in a blue moon! But come on! Don't dawdle! We really must hurry." Along a passage, the spark-man takes Rupert to

a window. "You've seen our Blue Moonshine, haven't you? Look, the moon is very low. When it sets, this castle vanishes until the next moonrise! So come along!" Flicking himself back into the corridor he leads the way to a handsome door, leans his tiny weight against it until it swings on well-oiled hinges, and Rupert enters a big room. To the little bear's surprise the two friendly children are already there facing a teacher and a blackboard.

RUPERT EXPLAINS TO TEACHER

"There's teacher," says the little man.
"Ask her to help. I think she can."

The teacher sees them standing there,
And says, "How are you, little bear?"

She adds, "These bits of pottery
Are like a vase that's owned by me."

So Rupert and the teacher fly
Through coloured air, which flickers by.

"That's the lady I've brought you to see," says the spark-man. "She's the sort of teacher you only meet once in a blue moon, never impatient, never hard to understand, never punishes anybody. I've given her those broken pieces, so go and meet her." The teacher has already seen him, and moves forward. "Ah, it's the little bear!" she says. "And those fragments of pottery are yours, eh? Come, let's examine them together." The teacher gazes closely at the bits of china while Rupert tells his story. "M'yes! I once had a pair of these," she says. "They were the only two of their kind. In one I used to keep pins, in the other Wishing Powder. Years ago, the second ornament disappeared, but how did it reach the shop you've just told me about?" As she speaks, the room quivers and fills with sparks. Hurriedly the teacher grabs Rupert's hand and they fly rather than walk through the swirling, coloured air while the very walls seem to wobble like jelly.

RUPERT SAYS THE WRONG THING

The teacher says, "I once had two,
So I will give this vase to you."

"Is it for me?" cries Rupert. "Oh!
It's far too rare for that, you know."

His words make teacher faint away
And Rupert stares – what did *he say?*

To ask for something not so rare,
No wonder teacher gasped for air!

A minute later Rupert finds himself in the teacher's study and up on the mantelshelf is a spill-holder exactly like the one he broke. "After coming so far, the little bear shall certainly have it for his daddy," she says, giving it to him. "Oh, *thank* you! How topping!" cries Rupert. "But isn't it very, very rare and precious? Couldn't I have just an ordinary one?" In his delight, he doesn't notice the effect his words have had on the teacher. When Rupert glances up, he sees to his astonishment that the teacher is lying on a couch and looking shocked. The little girl is patting her hand while the boy runs with smelling salts. Even the spark-man is shaken. "Oh dear, what's happened? Have I done something wrong?" Rupert whispers. "I should think you have!" exclaims the spark-man. "You asked for an *ordinary* spill-holder. Don't you know that *nothing* is ordinary in a Blue Moon? Nothing at all! The very idea made teacher faint."

RUPERT TRAVELS BACK ALONE

Then Rupert hears the spark-man shout,
"She'll be all right! Now let's go out!"

"You used your eiderdown before –
Jump on! I'll wish you home once more."

"I simply can't believe my eyes,
The castle's vanished!" Rupert cries.

So Rupert, gliding at a height,
Is carried safely through the night.

Now the air becomes thicker and distant rumblings are heard. "Come away!" cries the spark-man. "Leave teacher! She'll be all right by next moonrise, but you – you haven't a second to lose! The Blue Moon is setting, and we are all just going to vanish!" He dashes round a corner and there on the floor is Rupert's eiderdown and the paper bag, empty now except for a few grains of Wishing Powder. "Quick, I'll wish you home again!" squeaks the spark-man.

Rupert is just in the nick of time. Even as the spark-man throws his Wishing Powder, the walls of the great castle grow pale and disappear. Then the spark-man himself vanishes and Rupert is alone. But the good work has been done. Coloured clouds have begun to form and the eiderdown has risen into them. Soon it is travelling fast with Rupert sitting very still and feeling rather lonely in the sky without his tiny companion beside him.

RUPERT LANDS ON HIS OWN BED

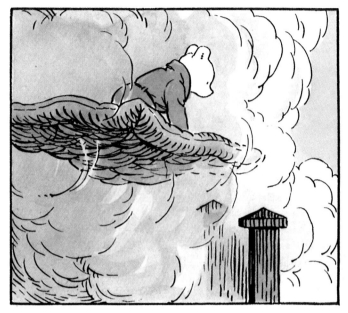

The eiderdown then slowly sinks.
"Ah, there's my bedpost," Rupert thinks.

"It seems I'm back in my own bed,"
Gasps Rupert, as he rubs his head.

"Now did I dream this all or not?
It's true, for here's the Blue-Moon pot."

Next morning, Rupert first prepares
The present, then he runs downstairs.

To Rupert's surprise this journey seems very short. No sooner has it got up speed than this strange craft begins to slow down, the cloud thins and below him he sees the dim shape of a bedpost. And now the eiderdown has slid over it, swung right round and settled down with hardly a quiver, leaving him exactly where he started from. The clouds silently roll away and Rupert holds his head. "Did all that really happen to me?" he whispers. "I feel quite dazed."

Before he takes off his dressing-gown, Rupert looks at the new spill-holder that is still on the eiderdown beside him. "Yes, it must all be true," he smiles. "B'rr! It's cold here. How odd that I didn't feel at all cold during that long journey!" He pops into bed and is soon fast asleep. In the morning he packs the present in lots of paper. He is so interested in this that he does not look at his own full stocking until his task is finished. Then he carries both into the sitting room.

RUPERT REMEMBERS THE FAIRY

His daddy says, "Oh, thank you, dear!
I wonder what you've wrapped up here?"

"It's beautiful!" cries Mr Bear.
"I'm sure it must be very rare."

"There's one thing missing, I can see.
A fairy for our Christmas tree."

Then Rupert hits upon a plan.
He means to try it, if he can.

Rupert empties his stocking before Mr Bear appears. Then he holds up his own parcel and watches in excitement as his daddy unwraps it. "But whatever is it?" says the puzzled Mr Bear. "I've never seen anything like it." "No, there isn't another like it," laughs Rupert. "It's a spill-holder, and it's only found once in a blue moon!" Mrs Bear, who has just come in, quickly makes some spills, and they all look at the gift again in delight. "It's just beautiful!" says Mr Bear.

Rupert tries to tell his daddy of his extraordinary journey to the castle of the Blue Moonshine, but Mr Bear continues to handle his present, and hardly seems to listen, so Rupert strolls away. "I believe he thinks I'm making up a fairy tale," he murmurs. "Fairy tale? That reminds me! Mummy said that the one thing she couldn't get was a fairy for the Christmas tree. It would look better if there was one." Gradually a wonderful idea comes to him.

RUPERT MAKES HIS PALS LAUGH

He finds some Wishing Powder grains,
And luckily enough remains.

"Mine's like a crown! Just fancy that!"
Laughs Podgy, trying on his hat.

Then Rupert's friends all gather round,
To hear how Daddy's vase was found.

"Oh, what a thrilling tale to tell!
You made it up extremely well!"

Following his new notion, Rupert runs back to his bedoom. "Good!" he breathes. "Mummy hasn't made my bed yet." He peers closely at his eiderdown. "Two lots of Wishing Powder have been thrown on this! Yes, yes! There's some left." Fetching another paper bag, he collects a little of it. "I'll try my plan this afternoon when Mummy's not busy," he decides. But when the afternoon arrives, his pals call on him earlier than expected, and he starts to welcome them.

First of all, Rupert brings a box of party caps for the friends who have come to wish him a happy Christmas. Then he gathers them in a circle and tells them of his adventures, from the beginning until the setting of the blue moon, and his lucky escape. His pals listen intently until he finishes. Then to his surprise they join in happy laughter. "Really, Rupert, you can't expect us to swallow all that!" cries Podgy. "What lovely adventures you do make up!" Willie chuckles.

RUPERT'S WISH COMES TRUE

"You don't believe my story, eh?
I'll prove it! That's all I can say!"

"This powder from the real Blue Moon
Will make my wish come true quite soon!"

High on the tree the fairy stands,
And all the playmates clap their hands.

Laughs Rupert, "Mummy, there you are –
Your fairy with a wand and star!"

Rupert rises and faces his friends. "Oh, so you don't believe my adventure, eh?" he says. "Well, here's some of the actual Wishing Powder in this bag. And did you all notice that our Christmas tree had no fairy on it? Now watch! I'm going to see if I've learned what the spark-man told me." Again, he tosses a little of the magic powder into the fire, this time wishing hard while he does so. Again stars and coloured lights swirl out and across the room. Turning anxiously, Rupert gives a cry of triumph. "Look, look! She's there! The fairy on the tree! *Now* do you believe my story was true?" And, sure enough, as the coloured mists swirl away out of the window, the dainty figure stands out clearly. Mrs Bear has entered in time to see what has happened, and she calls out in surprise. "The fairy is specially for you, Mummy!" says Rupert. "I knew that was what you wanted for Christmas. And now you must hear my story too!"

RUPERT'S SPILL-HOLDER AND THE SPARK-MAN

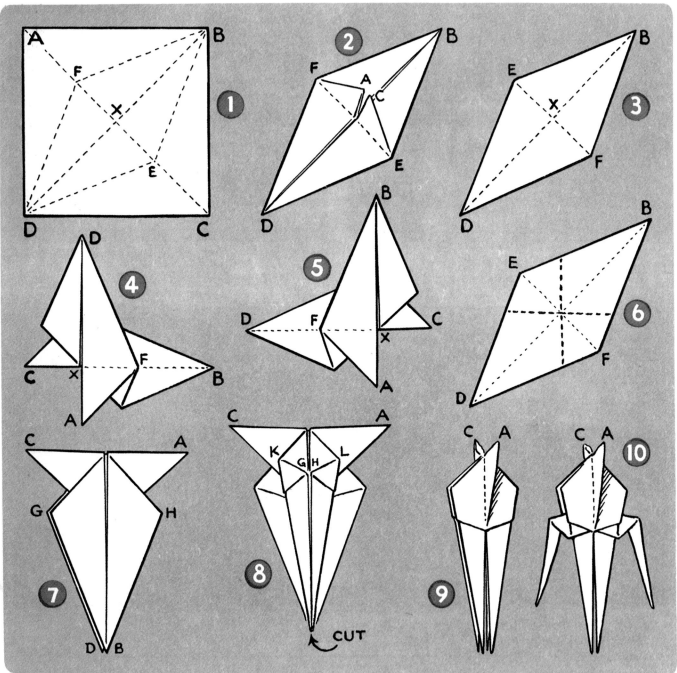

HOW TO MAKE RUPERT'S SPILL-HOLDER

Take a square of paper not less than 15 cm across and fold it corner to corner to give the crease BD. Turn it over and fold B to D to make the crease AC. Then put the four sides in turn to the line BD to make the folds BE, BF, DE and DF as in Figure 1. Now lay all four sides as far as possible to the line BD, leaving the points A and C sticking up (Figure 2). Turn the shape over (Figure 3) and fold it in half through the middle point X, so that the line XF lies exactly along XB as in Figure 4. Repeat the other way making XF lie along XD (Figure 5).

This gives you the two new creases shown in Figure 6. Press them firmly. Next carry E across to F, letting B come across to D, making Figure 7. Fold the sides BG and BH to the middle line and again press firmly (Figure 8). Repeat on the other side and, taking your scissors, cut from the point marked by the arrow, up the middle line more than halfway to the top to give the shape four 'legs'. Fold K to L and repeat the other side to make Figure 9. Give two of the legs double folds as in Figure 10, and repeat with the other two legs.

28

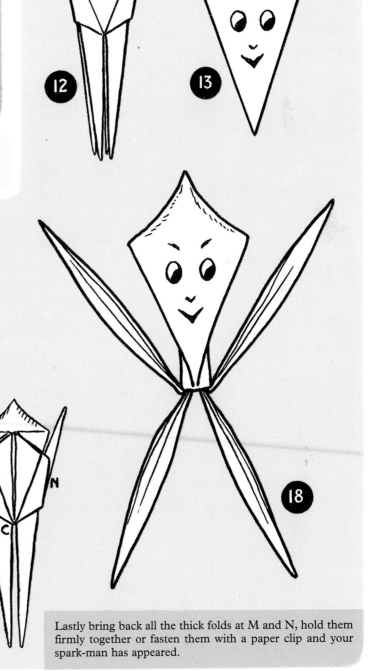

HOW TO MAKE THE SPARK-MAN

To make Rupert's spark-man take another square of paper and fold it in the same way up to Figure 9. Then press the point A back and flatten the shape as in Figure 12. On this new kite shape draw a cheery little face and pinch the upper sides to bring the head to a point (Figure 13). Lift the front 'legs', press them firmly upward to make arms (Figure 14) and turn the shape round, pressing the point C flat (Figure 15). Now comes a tricky fold as you take the point C as in Figure 16 and bring it down as far as it will go, working the sides in and pressing them neatly to look like Figure 17.

Bend the legs away from each other, open out the lily-like shapes at A and C and there is your spill-holder (Figure 11).

Lastly bring back all the thick folds at M and N, hold them firmly together or fasten them with a paper clip and your spark-man has appeared.

RUPERT and the

All four pals meant to start today
Their boat and camping holiday.

For weeks Rupert and Bingo with Algy Pug and Bill Badger have been planning a river camping holiday. They will explore the river by boat during the day and camp beside it each night. But they are just about to leave when Bill and Algy find a fault in their boat which must be put right. "We'll go ahead," Rupert says. "We shall camp tonight and wait for you to catch up tomorrow."

RIVER PIRATES

But Bill and Algy must delay
Their setting out until next day.

"That sun glint up there on the slope!
It's someone with a telescope."

So off row Rupert and Bingo, taking it easy for they don't want to get too far ahead. They have been going for only a little when Rupert spots something! "That flashing on the hill!" he says. "The sun is glinting on a telescope. Someone's watching us." Nearer they see that the watcher is a man. Then they see him close his telescope and signal to someone with a scarf or neckerchief.

Now they can see him signalling
With his 'kerchief or some such thing.

From the Rupert Annual, *1987. Illustrated by* John Harrold.

RUPERT'S BOAT ACTS STRANGELY

The river that's been smooth 'til now
Begins to swirl about their bow.

The boat is dragged, against their will,
Into the bank below the hill.

"We're going to hit!" the two pals wail.
Then in a tunnel thing they sail.

Now Rupert grabs a branch but – crack!
It snaps and he sprawls on his back.

"That's odd," Bingo muses. "Someone examines us through a telescope then starts signalling. Do you think it was about us?" But Rupert doesn't answer. He has noticed something just as strange – and more frightening. The water, smooth until now, is swirling round the boat in an alarming way. He digs the paddle in hard and tries to steer. "It's no use, Bingo!" he gasps. "I can't control the boat. We're being pulled into the bank!" Bingo gives a gasp of horror as the dense bushes and trees on the bank loom closer and closer. Rupert keeps trying to turn the boat. It is hopeless. Then, when it seems they are going to crash, the bushes part and they see they are being drawn into a low tunnel. Rupert drops the paddle, springs onto his seat and grabs an overhanging branch. For a moment the boat slows. Then … crr-a-ack … the branch snaps and Rupert goes sprawling in the boat.

RUPERT GOES THROUGH A TUNNEL

Rupert and Bingo hold on tight.
Ahead now they can see daylight.

Out of the tunnel worse awaits –
They're racing hard towards sluice gates!

"We're going to crash!" poor Bingo squeals.
Next moment they're head over heels!

They haven't crashed. Their bow has met
With such a holt, a winched-up net.

The rushing water booms inside the tunnel as Rupert and Bingo are swept along. Ahead they see a glimmer of light which grows fast as they race towards it. Then suddenly they are in daylight in a narrow channel with steep stone sides. But their feeling of relief lasts only a moment for they are still travelling at great speed. And just ahead of them is a very solid-looking sluice gate. Horrified, they watch it loom larger and larger. Then as it seems the boat must smash into the gate it stops with a jolt pitching the pals head over heels. The nose of the boat is pressed against a stout net which has sprung out of the water. "What on earth …?" Bingo gasps as he picks himself up. Rupert says nothing. He is staring at a figure on the bank. It is a very old pirate, brandishing a rusty cutlass. On the other side a second old pirate is securing the rope which pulled up the net.

RUPERT IS CAUGHT BY PIRATES

The shaken chums have, it appears,
Been trapped by ancient buccaneers.

Our two are hustled through a door,
Wondering what may lie in store.

The man named Ben says, "Here you'll stay
Until your parents ransom pay."

And now there comes into the mill
The one who signalled from the hill.

"Pull 'em in, Josh!" cries the old pirate as he totters across the top of the sluice gate. "Ay, ay, Ben," quavers the other and drags the pals' craft to the bank with a boathook. "Out ye get!" he cries. Rupert and Bingo scramble from the boat. They are speechless. Everything has happened so fast. "Into the mill!" pipes Ben and points with his sword at the building behind him. It is a deserted-looking place with a tunnel in the middle through which water races. The inside echoes with the sound of the water. "Oh, please," Rupert begs, "what do you want with us?" Ben, who seems to be in charge, points a shaky finger and croaks, "What we want is ransom! Ye're our prisoners and here you'll stay 'til your families pay ransom for ye." Just then the door opens and in comes yet another very old pirate. He is knotting a 'kerchief about his neck. "I'm sure he's the one we saw signalling," Bingo whispers.

RUPERT HEARS THE PIRATE PLAN

Ben tells him, "Tom, go up the stair
And in the big loft lock this pair."

"Too aged for the Spanish Main,"
Says Tom, "we three came home again."

"That tunnel ought to have a grille
So's boats don't get dragged to the mill."

"But we three took the grille away
As you two youngsters found today!"

"Young Tom, take the prisoners to the loft and lock 'em in," Ben orders the newcomer. Young Tom, who looks just as old as the others, ushers Rupert and Bingo up to a loft stretching the length of the mill. Even here the rumbling of the water is loud. "Do this, do that," grumbles Tom. "Like I was still a cabin boy. That Ben forgets 'twas my idea to use the old mill to trap boats. 'Tain't fair." "No it isn't," chorus Bingo and Rupert who want to keep Tom talking. Delighted to have someone

listen to him for a change, Tom tells the pals how he and the others decided to become river pirates when they got too old for pirating on the Spanish Main. He remembered the old mill and how its wheel was driven by water drawn from the river through a culvert when the sluice was opened wide. There was a grille or grating on it to stop boats been drawn in. "So I told 'em, remove the grating and we can pull in boats – and ransom prisoners," Tom gloats.

RUPERT FINDS A TRAPDOOR

"Rupert, somehow we must get free
And tell the police about those three."

To find a way the two explore,
And Rupert spots an old trapdoor.

"It's where the mill wheel used to be.
But wait! The water's slowing. See?"

They're winding shut, those aged two,
The sluice that lets the water through.

"Young Tom, stop wasting time up there," Ben calls from below. Tom pulls a face but he still scurries off, locking the door. "Rupert, now that we know what they're up to we must escape and tell the police," Bingo says. "Let's see if there's anything up here we can use." So the pals start poking about among old bits of mill equipment. Suddenly Rupert calls, "Look!" Bingo looks up from the things he has found to see his pal holding open an old trapdoor.

Next moment the two are peering at the mill-stream racing through the tunnel. "It's where the mill-wheel was," Bingo breathes. "You can see the axle stumps ... but wait! The water's slowing. They must be shutting the sluice." Rupert scrambles across to a window and looks out. Sure enough, Josh and Young Tom are winding shut the underwater 'doors' that let the stream in through the gate. And Tom is still complaining about being ordered around.

"It's now so quiet we're sure to know
When those three let the water flow."

Cries Bingo, "Here's some useful gear."
"Hush!" Rupert says. "They're coming here."

"You'll write your parents and you'll say
To get you back they'll have to pay."

And Ben goes on, "If you don't write
You'll have no supper here tonight."

When the pals lower the trapdoor they notice something – how quiet it is now that the water is not running. "We'll be able to tell any time they open the sluice," Bingo says. Before Rupert can ask why that's important Bingo goes on, "I have an idea for escaping. Some of this old stuff in here will be useful. You keep watch while I sort it out." A little later Bingo has to drag a tarpaulin over his bits and pieces when Rupert hisses, "They're coming up here!"

The door opens and in file the pirates. Ben is carrying paper and a quill pen. The pals, he announces, must write to their parents to say they won't be set free until ransom is paid. He tries to look fierce and says, "If ye don't ye shall have no supper!" "Ay, and we 'as good ones," pipes Josh. "Chips and jam sangwidges." Since they are planning to escape, anyway, the pals sign.. What's more, they're very hungry ... even for jam sandwiches with chips.

Continued on page 42.

RUPERT'S RANSOM NOTE

The pirates ask Rupert to write a ransom note to his parents – but Rupert has a better idea. He will write his letter in code so the pirates won't understand!

Can you decode Rupert's ransom note?
Use the key below to help you!

23	22	26	9		14	6	14	14	2		26	13	23
D	E	A	R		M	U	M	M	Y		A	N	D

23	26	23	23	2 ,		25	18	13	20	12		26	13	23
D	A	D	D	Y ,		B	I	N	G	O		A	N	D

18		26	9	22		25	22	18	13	20		19	22	15	23
I		A	R	E		B	E	I	N	G		H	E	L	D

19	12	8	7	26	20	22		26	7		7	19	22
H	O	S	T	A	G	E		A	T		T	H	E

12	15	23		14	18	15	15		18	13
O	L	D		M	I	L	L		I	N

13	6	7	24	19	22	8	7	22	9 !		8	12	8 !
N	U	T	C	H	E	S	T	E	R !		S	O	S !

15	12	5	22		9	6	11	22	9	7
L	O	V	E		R	U	P	E	R	T

Rupert's Secret Code Key												
A	B	C	D	E	F	G	H	I	J	K	L	M
26	25	24	23	22	21	20	19	18	17	16	15	14
N	O	P	Q	R	S	T	U	V	W	X	Y	Z
13	12	11	10	9	8	7	6	5	4	3	2	1

Answer on page 68.

RU-DOKU

To solve the puzzle, write the names of the pals in the empty frames, so that each line, column and 4x4 block contains only one of each chum.

BILL

ALGY

RUPERT

BINGO

ALGY

RUPERT

BINGO

Answer on page 68.

RUPERT'S HOLIDAY ADVENTURE

Rupert and his chums are looking forward to their sailing and camping holiday. Who will reach the campsite first?

Ask three friends to play with you. Choose who will be Rupert, Bingo, Bill and Algy. Find a dice and four counters to play with – you could use buttons or coins as counters. The first chum to roll a 6 starts the game, and the winner is the first to make it to the campsite.

START

1

2
You've forgotten warm clothing!
Miss 1 go.

3

17

16

15

14
You're heading ov
the rapids! **Whi:
forward 2 spac**

18

19
The pirates have caught you up and have cornered you!
Miss 1 go.

20

21
You escape and sail into a lovely open lake!
Row forward 2 spaces.

22

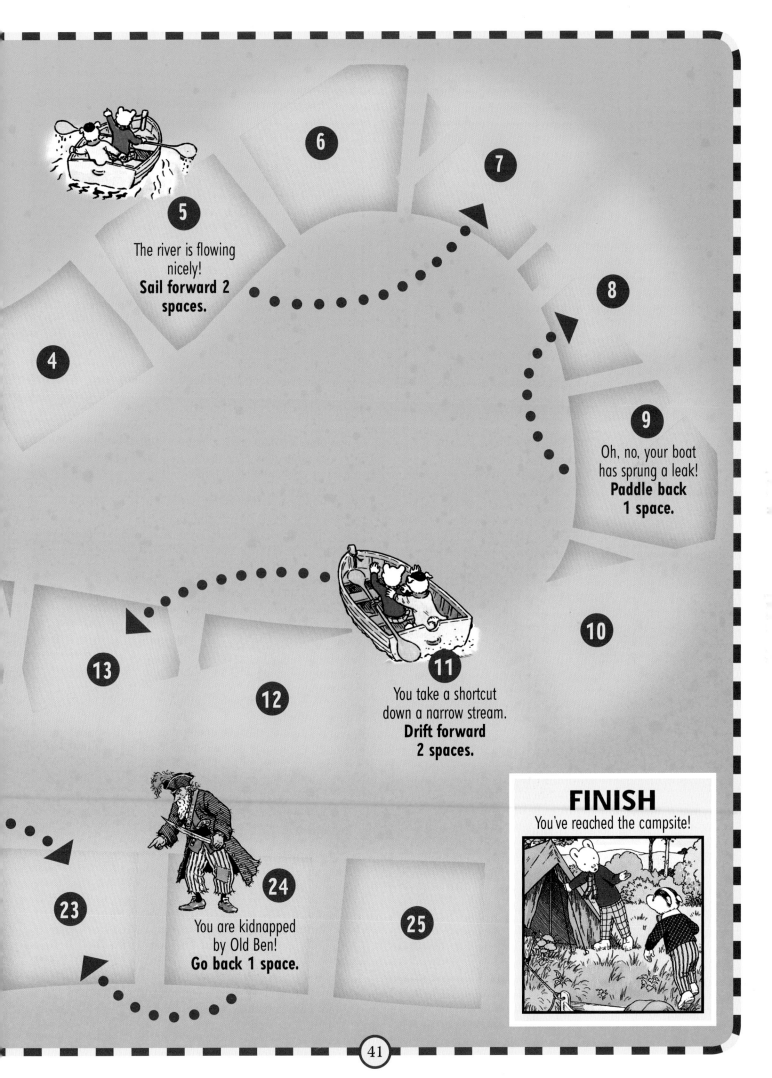

5
The river is flowing nicely!
Sail forward 2 spaces.

9
Oh, no, your boat has sprung a leak!
Paddle back 1 space.

11
You take a shortcut down a narrow stream.
Drift forward 2 spaces.

24
You are kidnapped by Old Ben!
Go back 1 space.

FINISH
You've reached the campsite!

Continued from page 37.

Rupert and the River Pirates

RUPERT'S PAL PLANS A RAFT

"The first of many ransom notes!
Now we'll start pulling in more boats."

"Now," Bingo says, "here's what we'll do
Next time they let the water through.

We'll make a raft, that is my scheme,
And lower it to the running stream."

They just have time to hide their gear
Before two of the men appear.

"They're awful pirates," Rupert thinks. "They haven't said how much ransom they want nor even got our addresses." But the old pirates seem happy enough. "The first o' many ransom notes!" Ben crows. "We'll be pulling boats in all the time now!" "That's what I wanted to know," says Bingo when the pirates have gone. "They'll have to open the sluice. That's what we need." And he whips the cover off the pile of old mill equipment he has found. His main find is a pallet that was used for lowering sacks of flour in the old days. With it are several oil cans, rope, twine and a pulley. Rupert sees at once what Bingo plans – a raft! "Right!" Bingo says. "We'll start it after supper when the pirates have gone to bed." As it is, they just have time to hide the things before supper arrives. "I've brought you a lamp," Josh says. "In case you don't like the dark." Plainly, he is trying hard not to sound kindly.

RUPERT HELPS WITH THE RAFT

When supper's done the pals set to.
There's such a lot they have to do.

At last it's done. They've made the raft,
A makeshift but a sturdy craft.

Now there remains just one thing more,
The means to lower it through the floor.

And now the pair are set to go
When they can hear the stream below.

Grateful for the light Josh brought, our two start work when supper has been cleared away. Using Bingo's pocket-knife they cut lengths of twine to tie oil cans to the pallet. "This will help to keep the raft afloat," Bingo whispers. Long past their usual bedtime the pals work on their raft. At last it is done. "That should do," Bingo says. "I think it's strong enough." "How do we get it into the water?" Rupert asks. "I've worked that out," says Bingo. "We lower it, as it used to be lowered with sacks of flour – except that we drop it through the trapdoor into the water when it's moving fast." So while Rupert ties lines to the rings on the pallet Bingo gets the pulley rigged. At last all is ready. They pull the tarpaulin over their craft and climb onto their mattresses. "We must be ready to go the first time they open the sluice gate and the water starts running again," Bingo says. "Goodnight, Rupert."

RUPERT SPIES ON THE PIRATES

The pals awake at break of day.
The men bring in their breakfast tray.

Young Tom's inclined to stay and chat,
But Ben says there's no time for that.

And off the pals soon see Tom trot
Towards his hilltop lookout spot.

"Tom's signalling to them below,"
Says Rupert. "Let's get set to go."

"Rise and shine!" Rupert and Bingo stir at the call to find a sunny morning and that the three old pirates have brought their breakfast – tea and bread spread with condensed milk. The pirates don't even glance at where the raft is hidden. Instead they watch the pals breakfast as if anxious they should enjoy it. Suddenly Ben turns on Tom: "Time's wasting. Off to your lookout post and watch for boats." The pals exchange a "get ready" look.

The pals listen to the pirates clattering downstairs then they go to the window. In a moment they see the pirates emerge from the mill. Ben and Josh settle themselves on a bench. Tom sets off for the hilltop, muttering to himself. For a long time nothing happens as Tom sweeps the river with his telescope. Suddenly Rupert calls urgently to Bingo who is checking the raft, "He's waving his scarf. He must have spotted a boat."

RUPERT GETS READY TO ESCAPE

The old men open up the gate
That sets the mill-stream in full spate.

The pals act fast. They rig the rope.
This is their chance to flee, they hope.

Now open up the old trapdoor.
My goodness, hear that water roar!

They're nervous but they cannot stay.
"Right," Rupert says. "Let's lower away."

As soon as Ben and Josh spot Tom's signal they totter to the sluice gate and start to wind it open. The pals spring into action. A rope fixed to the raft is fed through the pulley. Bingo climbs onto a box to hang the pulley from a hook over the trapdoor. Rupert leads the lowering rope through a ring on the floor. Everything is as ready as it can be. Above the clanking of the sluice being opened the pals hear water beginning to race through the tunnel.

They open the trapdoor. Now neither feels quite so brave. They gasp at the sight of the mill-stream racing and roaring beneath them. Can their makeshift craft really stand up to that sort of thing? Well, there's one way to find out. "Come on," says Bingo. "No point in waiting. Let's get it into the water." They let go the lowering line from its ring and take the weight of their raft. They ease it towards the opening. "Right, lower away!" Rupert says.

RUPERT HAS TO JUMP FOR IT

Just see that poor raft lurch and sway.
Brave Bingo says he'll lead the way.

It's Rupert's turn. He doesn't wait.
This is no time to hesitate.

He drops. He hangs on for dear life.
Now Bingo has got out his knife.

He saws the rope. It strains. It parts.
And down the stream the pals' raft darts.

Feeding out the line a little at a time, Rupert and Bingo at last have the raft on the water. "My plan, so I'll go first," Bingo says. Rupert secures the lowering line and Bingo climbs down it to the raft. He makes it! Now it is Rupert's turn. The rope he must climb down is jerking and bucking as the mill-stream tries to carry the raft away. Nothing for it! He takes a deep breath and launches himself at the wildly bucking rope.

Rupert manages to grab the rope but it is jerking so wildly that in order not to be smashed against the sides of the tunnel he has to let go. Down he plunges towards the racing mill-stream. Bingo grabs him as he drops and drags him onto the raft. "Hold tight!" he shouts and slashes at the rope with his knife. It parts. The raft leaps free and he sprawls beside Rupert, hanging on desperately as the raft goes bucketing along.

RUPERT RIDES THE MILL-STREAM

"I say," gasps Rupert, "what a ride!
Let's hope that we don't hit the side."

Then some way up ahead he sees
The mill-stream races into trees.

Below the trees it's gloomy green.
But wait! Now sunlight's to be seen.

"Well!" Bingo cries. "For goodness' sake!
I know this place – Nutchester Lake!"

The roaring mill-stream is so loud that the pals can't hear if the pirates have noticed their escape. Anyway, they're too busy hanging onto the raft. "Where do you think this goes?" Rupert gasps. "No idea!" Bingo shouts. "Let's hope we don't hit the sides and get wrecked." Rupert, who hasn't thought of this, gasps. Then they see ahead of them that the mill-stream disappears into a screen of trees. "Now what?" Rupert wonders.

Just then Bingo cries, "Look out! Branches!" He throws himself flat. So does Rupert, just in time to escape being swept from the raft by a low-hanging branch. The trees are so dense and close that sunlight can't get through and the pals are carried along in a greeny gloom. Not knowing what lies ahead is frightening. Then it begins to get lighter. The sunlight gets stronger and from somewhere ahead Rupert and Bingo hear a loud buzzing noise.

RUPERT IS RESCUED

A motorboat hoves into sight.
They hope the owner spots their plight.

He does, and takes the raft in tow.
"Now what's all this?" he wants to know.

He hears their tale then says, "Let's go
And tell the police. They ought to know."

"Can I believe this tale, you two?
I think I'll ring and check on you."

"Nutchester Lake!" exclaims Bingo. And there ahead is the source of the buzzing sound – a motorboat! "Ahoy!" the pals shout and from the motorboat's cabin a man appears. He stars then turns his boat towards them. "It's silly to play out here on a raft ..." he begins. "But we're not playing!" Rupert protests. "We're escaping from pirates!" "Pirates!" the man repeats. "Now that's enough of your nonsense." "Oh, please, we are telling the truth!" Rupert pleads. The pals sound so earnest that at last the man takes them in tow, saying that he is taking them to the police station to tell their story.

The policeman who hears their tale does not seem to believe it. "You come from Nutwood, eh?" he frowns. "I know PC Growler there. I shall ring and ask him about you. Pirates, indeed! What will some of you youngsters think of next!" And with that he dials the number of Nutwood police station. The pals wait anxiously.

RUPERT HELPS THE POLICE

*"Your village bobby says that I
Should take your word. You never lie."*

*So in the police car off they go
To let the river bobbies know.*

*The pals are asked to show the way.
"A police boat ride! Of course!" they say.*

*Tom's seen them, waved, the waters race.
They're dragged towards the tunnel place.*

"H'm, is that a fact?" The policeman listens to PC Growler in Nutwood. He puts down the phone. "Well," he says, "it seems that neither of you tells lies, so I've got to believe this extraordinary tale about pirates on the river. Oh, dear! What are the River Police going to say about this? Well, come on! Let's go and find out." With that he leads the pals out to his police car and sets off for the Nutchester River Police station.

The River Police act at once when they hear what has happened to Rupert and Bingo. Will Rupert and Bingo come with them and show just where they were trapped in their boat? Of course! Who's going to turn down the chance of a trip in a River Police boat? So off they go. As they get near the tunnel leading to the mill Rupert and Bingo spot Young Tom at his lookout post. Already he is signalling. "Look out!" Rupert calls. Too late. The water is swirling!

RUPERT FINDS HIS PALS

"Quick, duck your heads. The roof is low!"
Too late. Police helmets flying go.

Up comes the net. Ben groans, "Oh, dear!
We've really caught the wrong lot here."

Tom rushes down to see his prize,
Gets close and can't believe his eyes.

Then at a window Rupert spies
Two faces. "They're our pals!" he cries.

Before the policemen know what's happening their boat is being dragged into the tunnel. "Watch your heads!" Rupert cries. Again too late. Helmets go flying! The police boat is swept through the tunnel by the current. This time Rupert and Bingo know what to expect and they are ready for the shock when the net brings the craft to a jolting halt. Being large and heavy the two policemen avoid being sent sprawling. There is a long silence.

Ben breaks the silence. "Oh, dear," he squeaks. "We've really caught the wrong lot here!" Just then Tom hurries down to see what he's trapped. For an awe-stricken moment he regards the scene. "I really must get glasses," he says at last.

It is while the pirates are being rounded up that Rupert happens to look up at the loft windows. "Bingo!" he cries. "Look who's there!" Grinning down at them from the loft they left such a short time ago are – Bill and Algy.

RUPERT MAKES A PLEA

Algy explains that Bill and he
Were captured as their pals got free.

Then off the police – and pirates – go
With Rupert and his chums in tow.

Now Rupert asks the policeman, "Please
Don't punish them." And he agrees.

As once again our chums set out,
"Good luck and thanks!" the pirates shout.

"Bill! Algy!" Rupert and Bingo run to greet the two captives who have just been let out of the loft. "They caught us just as you and Bingo were escaping," laughs Algy. "They seemed quite upset that you'd gone after they'd given you supper and the like." "I know," Rupert says. "They're awful pirates because they're kind." Just then one of the policemen calls, "Back to Nutchester." And off they go, the police boat with the pirates in it, towing the other two.

At the River Police station Rupert goes up to one of the policemen. "They're not really bad," he begins. "I know," says the policeman. "We'll find a place for them in the Rocky Bay Home for Retired Pirates." So Rupert and the others can set out again quite happily. As they leave, the old pirates wave after them. "Good luck!" they call. "Have a good holiday and do come and see us sometime."

RUPERT AT THE STATION

"How strange!" says Rupert, half aloud, while he stands waiting in the crowd.
"That poster isn't right, I'm sure. I've never seen those names before."

All has been hustle and bustle at Mr Bear's cottage, for he has decided to take his small family for a week's holiday in Cornwall. When the day arrives they are up very early, and Rupert finds it hard to sit still while he eats his breakfast. At last they are on their way, and after taking the bus to the town of Nutchester, they arrive at the station. Mr Bear buys the tickets at the booking office while Rupert waits nearby with his mummy and looks at all the things around him. Suddenly he sees a poster on the wall, and he stares at it with a frown.

"Surely those aren't the names of real seaside places," he murmurs. "I've never heard of them."

After puzzling over the names, it dawns on the little bear that the letters of each seaside town have been jumbled up. "Yes, I believe I can solve the first one …" he begins, but his thoughts are interrupted as his daddy shows him the tickets for the journey.

Help Rupert unscramble the names of these real seaside towns!

Answers on page 68.

RUPERT

and the
Bosun's Chair

Story devised and illustrated by Stuart Trotter.

For Rupert's half-term holiday
The Bears escape to Castle Bay.

The Bears' landlady tells the pair,
"My friend, Lord Lachlan, he lives there!"

"The lord must have a splendid view,"
Thinks Rupert. "But then, I do, too!"

"I shan't be far," says Rupert Bear.
"I'll just be playing over there."

It's spring half-term, and Rupert's mummy is taking him to Castle Bay.

At the Bed and Breakfast where they are staying, the landlady, Mrs Mugwell, tells him, "Lord Lachlan owns the castle on the rock. On a clear day, you can see for miles from the turret!" "Might I be able to visit?" Rupert asks. "It depends on the tides," she replies. "At low tide, you can walk across the sand to the island. But be careful, the tides move very quickly here."

Rupert gathers up his fishing net and an empty jam jar, and runs back outside. He tries to imagine the view from the castle turret. "It must be spectacular," he thinks, although his own view of the castle on the rock is quite superb!

Rupert picks his way down to the beach. "Don't stray out too far," says Mrs Bear. "Remember what Mrs Mugwell said about the tides." "I won't," Rupert promises. "I'll play close by." And off he scampers to play among the rock pools.

RUPERT HEARS OF A SEAL IN TROUBLE

A rock pool is a treasure trove
For little bears who love to rove!

But Rupert has some company –
A seagull with a warning plea.

"Your nets are causing trouble, Bear.
See that poor seal trapped over there!"

Across the outcrop Rupert spots
A seal all tangled up in knots!

The rock pools are full of tiny creatures and Rupert is so engrossed that at first he doesn't notice the anxious cawing of a seagull perched on the rocks nearby. "Won't you help?" squawks the bird eventually, and Rupert is startled to hear the gull speak. "Help who?" wonders Rupert. "Oh, it's all the same to you," the bird blusters. "You people come here wielding your nets, and have no consideration whatsoever. There's a seal in trouble, and you haven't lifted a finger to help!"

The bird soars away across the rocks. Rupert follows it with his eyes, and sure enough, sees a seal some yards away. The seal is wriggling strangely, and Rupert sees that the creature is tangled quite hopelessly in a trawler net. "That's terrible!" Rupert exclaims. "Of course I'll help!"

Carefully, Rupert clambers along the outcrop towards the seal. The poor creature grunts in discomfort, but Rupert calls out soothingly, "I'm coming to help you. Do keep still!"

RUPERT RESCUES THE SEAL

A trawler's net has bound him tight!
But Rupert soon puts things all right.

"Whenever you need help at sea,"
The seal assures him, "there I'll be!"

As Rupert Bear waves from the bay,
The seal turns tail and glides away.

But where's the beach? "Oh, help!" he cries.
"I didn't see the water rise!"

It takes Rupert some time to reach the seal on foot. The seagull perches nearby and taps its claw impatiently on the rocks as Rupert begins to untangle the seal from the trawler net. The poor animal is bound quite tightly, but with great patience Rupert is able to unwrap him from his bindings.

Once free, the seal barks gratefully at Rupert. "I am at your service," he tells the little bear. "If ever you need help at sea, call, and I'll be there."

"It was no trouble," Rupert assures the seal. The creature slides away over the rocks, and into the sea. Rupert waves goodbye, then begins to plot his route back to shore.

But he has forgotten to heed Mrs Mugwell's warning! The tide has come in while he's been helping the seal – and now he is stuck on the outcrop! Across the bay he can see the B & B, and the dock further in the distance. He has come out much farther than he meant to!

RUPERT MEETS JASPER

He picks his way along the shore.
The castle's closer than before.

The steps are steep and slippery,
So Rupert climbs them carefully.

The lord's son, Jasper, hears his plight
And offers him a bed that night.

But first the grounds must be explored,
And Rupert wants to meet the lord.

A thought strikes him, then, and he looks over his shoulder. The castle looms large behind him. He need only hop over a few more rocks before he reaches the island.

Rupert picks his way to the foot of a tall stone staircase that leads to the castle. Years of sea water have made the stones slippery, and Rupert must take great care as he climbs.

Once at the top, Rupert raps on a wooden door, and prepares to explain himself to Lord Lachlan.

But the door opens to reveal a small boy in a charming, old-fashioned buttoned tunic. He introduces himself as Jasper, Lord Lachlan's son. Rupert explains that he has been trapped by the tide. But, "Never mind, that happens a lot," Jasper says with a shrug. "You can stay the night, if you like. I'll show you around." Rupert is grateful, but keen to ask the lord's permission in person. So Jasper leads Rupert out through a vast courtyard, and into the turret.

RUPERT SEES THE STORM ROLL IN

Lord Lachlan rings the B & B –
"Tell Mrs Bear her son's with me."

Says Jasper, "Now what we should do
Is climb the tower and see the view!"

Then, up the steep and winding stairs
The little boy named Jasper tears.

A dark cloud rolls in suddenly
And starts a heavy storm at sea!

A friendly-looking man in a waistcoat and tails is busying himself in the turret when Jasper brings Rupert to meet him. Rupert tells his sorry tale to Lord Lachlan, but the man chuckles kindly and assures Rupert that he is welcome to stay the night. He telephones Mrs Mugwell, and asks his friend the landlady to let Mrs Bear know that Rupert is safe with him.

"Would you like to see the view from the turret?" Jasper asks Rupert.

"Oo, I'd love to! Rupert says, keenly. Before he can say another word, Jasper has hot-footed it up the winding spiral staircase. Rupert is still rather worn out from climbing up to the castle, and he follows some way behind.

As Rupert reaches the top of the tower, his excitement at seeing the view turns to disappointment when he spots a huge grey cloud drifting towards the island, bringing with it the threat of a flash storm.

RUPERT OFFERS TO HELP

A pleasure steamer is on course
To hit the rocks with quite some force!

The lighthouse needs its bulb replaced.
"I'll do it!" Rupert says with haste.

So to the cliff edge three pals tear –
There isn't any time to spare.

The lord rigs up the frail old Chair –
"It should just hold you, little bear."

In no time at all, the sky darkens, the winds rage, and the waves lash below. Through the rain, Rupert spots a pleasure steamer, forging its way through the choppy sea. Something isn't right – the steamer should be heading for the docks, but it's right on course to collide with the rocks! Rupert and Jasper run back down the stairwell and in one breath Rupert tells Lord Lachlan what he has seen. "The lighthouse lantern can't be working," the lord says, with worry.

"We must replace the bulb straight away." "May I go to the lighthouse?" Rupert asks. "If you're careful you may," Lord Lachlan replies. "You will have to take the Bosun's Chair."
Lord Lachlan runs to fetch a spare lightbulb, and packs it tightly in a waterproof satchel. Then he, Rupert and Jasper speed through the storm to the cliff edge, where the davit for the Bosun's Chair is set up. "This old Chair is just strong enough for one person," the lord warns Rupert.

RUPERT TAKES THE BOSUN'S CHAIR

Lord Lachlan lifts the little bear
Onto the swaying Bosun's Chair.

The waves below cause Rupert fright.
He grips the ropes with all his might.

It's been a rather scary ride,
But Rupert's reached the other side.

With trouble, as the storm winds roar,
He pushes in the metal door.

Lord Lachlan attaches the Bosun's Chair to the davit, then lifts Rupert onto the device. It has no harness or belt, so Rupert must grip the ropes tightly at all times.

The lord releases the Chair, and with alarming speed it zips along the guide ropes towards the lighthouse. The wind buffets the rigging, sending the Chair swinging to and fro. Rupert's excitement turns to worry as the ropes creak above him, and the waves lash below!

Rupert is relieved to feel the winch hitting the pulley at the lighthouse end. He grips the railings for dear life, and hoists himself onto the balcony, leaving the Chair swinging on its ropes.

Rupert walks around the balcony until he finds a diamond-shaped metal door amongst the window panes, leading into the service room. The wind pounds against the little bear as he pushes with all his might until it gives way and he is able to clamber inside.

RUPERT RESTORES THE LIGHT

"I can't believe a bulb so small
Can stop disaster in a squall!"

He swaps the bulb, turns on the light.
The lighthouse beam is once more bright!

Then Rupert leaves the service room
And sees the beam cut through the gloom.

He climbs aboard the Bosun's Chair
And launches off with extra care.

Rupert reaches into the satchel and pulls out the spare bulb. He can't believe something so small can reflect so much light across the seas and avert disaster!

Rupert unscrews the dead bulb and slips it into his satchel, before twisting the new bulb into place. He hits a trip switch and bright light floods out of the lantern. Rupert hopes that the steamer sees the light in time, and is able to change its course.

Rupert wriggles back out of the metal door onto the balcony again. The Bosun's Chair sways back and forth in the gale, and the wooden seat is saturated with saltwater. "Oh dear, perhaps I shouldn't have left the Chair outside," thinks Rupert. But there is no time to worry. He needs to return to the castle, to Lord Lachlan and Jasper. Rupert clambers over the balcony, grips the Chair with all his might, climbs aboard, and pushes himself away from the lighthouse.

But with a SNAP the ropes give way!
Old age has caused them both to fray.

As Rupert falls into the sea,
He calls for help, though hopelessly.

Then through the fathoms swims a friend
To save him from a watery end!

Upon the seal's back, safe once more,
The little bear rides to the shore.

The journey back towards the island is even more treacherous than the journey out. The wind lurches the Chair forward much faster than the rigging can possibly move it. The old ropes beneath Rupert's hands are damp from the sea spray, and suddenly, with a tired SNAP! both give way! Rupert is sent plummeting into the freezing, choppy seawater.

Between the icy water and the huge waves, Rupert is unable to swim back to the surface.

Rupert calls out for help, though the storm is still raging so loudly that he doesn't believe he'll be heard.

But somebody *has* heard his cries. Rupert's new friend, the seal, sees the little bear suspended in the water, and glides through the depths to his rescue. Rupert is delighted to see the seal's whiskery face. The seal helps Rupert slide onto his back. They race up to the surface of the water, then coast the waves towards the bay.

And when at last they see the sand
He's quite relieved to reach dry land!

He waves goodbye, and makes his way
Back to the safety of the bay.

At last the pleasure steamer's docked!
Though Rupert's mummy looks quite shocked.

"I thought the ship would run aground –
But everybody's safe and sound!"

The storm subsides, and the evening sky shifts from ominous black to peaceful blue once more, as the seal brings Rupert safely back to the beach. "Thank you!" Rupert calls out, but the seal has already disappeared back into the ocean.

The sea calms, and it is almost as if the storm never happened! Rupert races back up the beach, clambers over the rocks, and onto dry land again.

With a loud blast, the pleasure steamer comes in to dock.

Rupert is thrilled that the steamer has made it back safely. His adventure on the Bosun's Chair has been worthwhile.

"Rupert!" Mrs Bear hurries along the dockside towards her son. She looks terribly worried. "I thought you were staying at the castle tonight! Where have you been? And why are your clothes soaking wet?" "Well ..." But Rupert does not know where to begin in telling his mother everything that has happened in just one evening!

COLOUR IN RUPERT

Rupert has rescued the friendly seal from a trawler net. Now the seal is promising Rupert that he will always look out for the little bear at sea.

Using the small picture as a guide, colour in the big picture of Rupert and the seal as neatly as you can.

Don't forget to make Rupert's pullover red, and his scarf yellow!

SPOT THE DIFFERENCE

Mrs Bear is relieved to see Rupert safe after his adventure on the Bosun's Chair!
There are 10 differences between these two pictures
of Rupert meeting his mummy at the dock.
Can you spot them all?

Answers on page 68

RUPERT'S MEMORY TEST

1 What colour was Mrs Bear's scarf?

2 What could Rupert see on the island?

3 Who was watching Rupert?

4 What was in Rupert's jar?

5 Who was Rupert waving at?

6 How many buckles were on Jasper's tunic?

7 What was Rupert pointing at?

8 What colour was the lighthouse?

9 What was Rupert holding in his right hand?

10 How many creatures saw Rupert fall?

11 Who was carrying Rupert back to shore?

12 How many portholes were visible on the steamer?

Try this memory test only when you have read the whole story. Each of the pictures above is taken from the story Rupert and the Bosun's Chair. Study them carefully, then see if you can answer the questions.

Answers on page 68.

ANSWERS TO PUZZLES

p38, RUPERT'S RANSOM NOTE

Rupert's ransom note reads

DEAR MUMMY AND DADDY,

BINGO AND I ARE BEING HELD
HOSTAGE AT THE OLD MILL IN
NUTCHESTER. SOS!

LOVE RUPERT

p39, RU-DOKU

The completed grid should look like this:

a. Algy, b. Bingo, c. Algy, d. Rupert,
e. Bingo, f. Bill, g. Rupert.

p52, RUPERT AT THE STATION

The seven jumbled names that Rupert
sees are: BRIGHTON, TENBY,
POLPERRO, BARMOUTH, MARGATE,
LLANDUDNO and MORECAMBE.

p65, SPOT THE DIFFERENCE

One porthole is missing, the lifeboat is
a different colour, the woman's formerly
brown boots are red, the man holding his
hand to his head is missing, the seagull is
missing, Mrs Bear's umbrella is blue, the
hatch is missing from the office window,
Rupert's satchel is missing, the castle is
back-to-front and the tree on the island
is missing.

p66, RUPERT'S MEMORY TEST

1. Mrs Bear's scarf was yellow.

2. Rupert saw the castle on the island.

3. A seagull was watching Rupert.

4. A crab was in Rupert's jar.

5. Rupert was waving at the seal.

6. There were three buckles on Jasper's tunic.

7. Rupert was pointing at the pleasure steamer.

8. The lighthouse was striped red and white.

9. Rupert was holding a lightbulb.

10. Two creatures saw Rupert fall – the seal, and a fish.

11. The seal was carrying Rupert back to shore.

12. Two portholes were visible on the steamer.

A MUST FOR RUPERT FANS

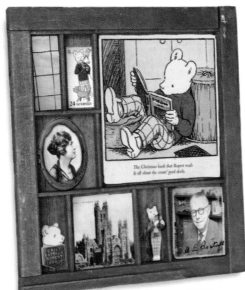

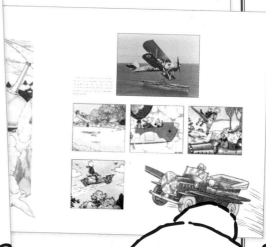

ISBN: 978 1 4052 5330 7   £25.00

This beautifully presented book is the fascinating story of how one little bear became a national treasure. It begins with Rupert's first appearance in the Express newspaper and follows his journey to the present day, highlighting the authors and illustrators who have helped bring Rupert Bear to life.

www.egmont.co.uk

EGMONT